# Just So

**by Jan Silverman**

**Music by Louise Lanzilotti**

**Baker's Plays**
c/o Samuel French, Inc.
45 West 25th Street
New York, NY 10010
bakersplays.com

# MUSIC USE NOTE

Licensees are solely responsible for obtaining formal written permission from copyright owners to use copyrighted music in the performance of this play and are strongly cautioned to do so. If no such permission is obtained by the licensee, then the licensee must use only original music that the licensee owns and controls. Licensees are solely responsible and liable for all music clearances and shall indemnify the copyright owners of the play and their licensing agent, Baker's Plays, against any costs, expenses, losses and liabilities arising from the use of music by licensees.

*JUST SO* was first performed at Temple University on October 31, 1981, under the direction of Jan Silverman, with the following cast:

**KIPLING/PYTHON/PARSEE/DJINNI/CAT** . . . . . . . . . . . . Jay Hoover

**HIPPO/MOTHER JAGUAR/**
    **BIG GOD NQONG/WOMAN** . . . . . . . . . . . . . . . . Karen Tonjes

**OSTRICH/YELLOW DOG DINGO/**
    **TORTOISE/DOG** . . . . . . . . . . . . . . . . . . . . . . . . . . Diane DiJosie

**GIRAFFE/KANGAROO/RHINOCEROS/MAN** . . . . . . . . . . . . . . . . . . .
Richard Mailman

**ELEPHANT'S CHILD/COW/LITTLE JAGUAR**
    **/LITTLE GOD NQA** . . . . . . . . . . . . . . . . . . . . . . . . . .Donna Foley

**KOLOKOLO BIRD/CROCODILE/MIDDLE GOD NQUING**
    **/PORCUPINE/HORSE** . . . . . . . . . . . . . . . . . . . . . Nina Hodoruk

**THE CAMEL** was played on alternate performances by Matthew Jones and Oberon Benasutti

# CHARACTERS

*(In order of appearance)*

**KIPLING**

**CAMEL**

**ELEPHANT'S CHILD**

**OSTRICH**

**GIRAFFE**

**HIPPOPOTAMUS**

**KOLOKOLO BIRD**

**PYTHON**

**CROCODILE**

**KANGAROO**

**LITTLE GOD NQA**

**MIDDLE GOD NQUING**

**BIG GOD NQUONG**

**YELLOW DOG DINGO**

**PARSEE**

**RHINOCEROS**

**MOTHER JAGUAR**

**LITTLE JAGUAR (DOFFLES)**

**PORCUPINE**

**TORTOISE**

**DJINNI**

**MAN**

**WOMAN**

**DOG**

**HORSE**

**COW**

**CAT**

Producers desiring a smaller cast can explore doubling. In the original production the double casting broke down as follows:

**KIPLING/PYTHON/PARSEE/DJINNI/CAT**

**HIPPO/MOTHER JAGUAR/BIG GOD NQONG/WOMAN**

**OSTRICH/YELLOW DOG DINGO/TORTOISE/DOG**

**GIRAFFE/KANGAROO/RHINOCEROS/MAN**

**ELEPHANT'S CHILD/COW/LITTLE JAGUAR/LITTLE GOD NQA**

**KOLOKOLO BIRD/CROCODILE/MIDDLE GOD NQUING/PORCUPINE/ HORSE**

**THE CAMEL**

## ABOUT THE PLAY

*JUST SO* should be presented as simply as possible, in a spirit of fun, inviting the audience to join in the pretending. Emphasis should be on actor-audience interaction, and the physical and vocal creativity of the cast.

The set for the original Temple University Children's Theatre production consisted of a series of sturdy wooden boxes constructed on an 18" module. There were four cubes, two rectangular boxes (18" x 18" x 9")one half cube (18" x 18" x 9"), and one very low platform which served as the bank of the Limpopo River. They were painted in bright, jungle-like colors. The set pieces were moved by the actors in full view of the audience, providing for a continuous flow of action. A transparent scrim hung upstage, allowing for projected effects, such as the Kangaroo's silhouette as he jumped, and a palm tree, as well as intense color washes.

The costumes were basic. Actors wore sweatpants, T-shirts and sneakers in colors appropriate to the characters they played. The actress playing the Kolokolo Bird and the Crocodile wore green; the Camel wore tan, and so forth. To these were added suggestive costume pieces that could be easily donned and removed. The Ostrich, for example, wore a tutu (right over her sweatpants!), and a stocking cap, the Python wore a long, striped sack and actually wriggled across the stage floor without the use of his arms; the Crocodile wore a green headband, from which dangled long Bo Derek braids done with green beads, and green gloves. The elephant's child wore a specially constructed head mask which, while showing the actor's face, featured elephant ears and a trunk which rolled up to create a bulbous nose. During the struggle with the crocodile, the nose was pulled out and unrolled to become the trunk.

# THE STORIES

*This play is dedicated to*
*my children*
*Allison & Jason*
*my grandchildren*
*Claire, Nathan, Leo & Alexandra*
*and my husband*
*Leon*

# PROLOGUE

*(The stage is dark. Light comes up on* **KIPLING**. *He is relaxed, seated or standing at ease. Blocks and other actors are onstage but in dim light. The mood is warm, thoughtful, mellow.)*

**KIPLING.** The beginnings of things. First times. How, for example, this hand – became a hand. Or how this box – got to be a box after starting out life as a tree. Or how I – Rudyard Kipling, traveler, storyteller – got to be so full of wondering. *(movement, lightening mood, increasing tempo)* But I could never wonder like a sensible man – or, at any rate, the way people say a sensible man should wonder. I wonder about things that end up making me smile – like, for instance, how the elephant got his long, long trunk. It looks like somebody just took hold and pulled! Or – how the camel got his hump, or how the Rhinoceros – got such a wrinkly skin and such a bad temper. *(He makes a scowly face.)* Or how you – *(to a child in the audience)* got such beautiful *(blond, black, red, brown, etc.)* hair. And then all the things I wonder about come and live inside my head until I just have to get them out! I mean, how would you like to have a rhinoceros inside your head? What a racket he makes! So I get them all out by putting them someplace else. I put them – into stories. And in the stories I answer my own questions, in my own way. What's inside my head today? An elephant, a kangaroo, a jaguar, a crocodile, a tortoise!

*(The animals are shaped by* **KIPLING** *as he goes to each actor.)*

And the camel – has anybody seen my camel?

*(Animals say "no" in their various personae.)*

Well, maybe he'll turn up.

**FULL COMPANY.** *(singing)* *

> HOW DID THE CAMEL GET HIS HUMP, I'D REALLY LIKE TO
>    KNOW:
> DID HE ALWAYS HAVE THAT LUMP SO MANY YEARS AGO?
> I'LL TELL YOU NOW IF YOU'LL COME WITH ME
> AND OPEN UP YOUR EYES,
>    I SURMISE
>    THAT IT HAPPENED
>    JUST SO!
> HOW DID THE ELEPHANT GET HIS TRUNK, I'D REALLY LIKE
>    TO KNOW
> AND HOW DID THE RHINO GET HIS SKIN,
> IT HANGS LIKE ROLLS OF DOUGH!
> I'LL TELL YOU NOW IF YOU'LL COME WITH ME
> AND OPEN UP YOUR EARS.
>    IT APPEARS
>    THAT IT HAPPENED
>    JUST SO!
> WHY IS THE DOGGIE MAN'S BEST FRIEND, WHO SLEEPS ON A
>    COZY SHELF,
> WHILE THE MOUSE IS WOMAN'S ENEMY, AND THE CAT JUST
>    WALKS
>    BY HIMSELF?
> OH, HOW DID THE ANIMALS GET SO STRANGE
> BEFORE THEY CAME TO THE ZOO?
> I'VE GOT SOME EXPLANATIONS, BUT THEY'RE NOT
>    NECESSARILY TRUE.
> I'LL TELL YOU NOW, IF YOU'LL COME WITH ME
> MY TONGUE IS IN MY CHEEK
>    JUST LAST WEEK
>    IT ALL HAPPENED
>    JUST SO!

### *HUMP SAYS THE CAMEL. – PART ONE*

*(Break from song into animal characters. One person becomes the **CAMEL**, enters, and looks disdainfully around.)*

**CAMEL.** Humph! *(walks off)*

---

* For music see page 50.

**FIRST ACTOR.** Who was that?

**KIPLING.** That's my camel! He lives all alone in the middle of the howling desert.

**SECOND ACTOR.** Just the place for him – he's a howler himself!

**FIRST ACTOR.** What's a howler?

**SECOND ACTOR.** A terrible mistake!

**KIPLING.** Yes! And he never does any work. He's most 'scruciatingly idle!

**FIRST ACTOR.** I heard he just eats sticks and thorns and pickles!

**CAMEL.** *(sticking his head in for a moment)* Humph!

**ALL OTHER ACTORS.** Go away!

*(He does, pursued by all but the* **ELEPHANT'S CHILD***, who takes centerstage and begins, having been encouraged and placed there by* **KIPLING***, who then exits.)*

### *"THE ELEPHANT'S CHILD"*

**ELEPHANT.** In the High and Far-Off Times, the Elephant had no trunk. He had only a blackish, bulgy nose that he could wriggle from side to side… *(He demonstrates.)* But he couldn't pick up things with it. There was one Elephant – an Elephant's Child… *(He becomes the elephant's child.)* And I am full of 'satiable curtiosity. That means I ask ever so many questions.

*(***OSTRICH** *enters, struts, preens, then sees something approaching offstage. She gives a cry of alarm, then buries her head in the sand. The* **ELEPHANT** *speaks without turning his head to look at the* **OSTRICH***.)*

Good morning, Aunt Ostrich.

*(approaches, looking at* **OSTRICH'S** *rump, then taps her on the shoulder)*

Aunt Ostrich?

**OSTRICH.** *(startled, jumps up, then is annoyed)* What do you want? Can't you see I'm hidden?

ELEPHANT. Oh Aunt Ostrich, why do you stick your head in the sand? It looks very funny, Aunt Ostrich, and why do you say you're hidden when I can see you very plainly, Aunt Ostrich and oh, Aunt Ostrich, just look at your tail feathers, and could you tell me, why do your tail feathers grow just so? *(All this in one breath.)*

OSTRICH. Questions, questions, questions! Here's that, for your 'satiable curtiosity! *(She smacks him and struts off.)*

ELEPHANT. Ohhhh!

*(He rubs his backside and looks off resentfully at* **OSTRICH**. *Enter Uncle* **GIRAFFE**.*)*

GIRAFFE. Good morning, Elephant's Child. *(He is tall and vain.)*

ELEPHANT. Good morning, Uncle Giraffe.

*(***GIRAFFE*** carefully combs his hair, using a pocket mirror, then smiles lovingly at himself in the mirror. He finds a tall branch and begins eating his breakfast.)*

Oh, Uncle Giraffe, why are you eating that top branch? Are the leaves really better up on the top, is that why you like them, or would it really just hurt your neck to bend down to get the low ones and how come your neck is so long anyway, can you tie it in a knot? Did you ever try, and what makes your skin so spotty?

GIRAFFE. Spotty? SPOTTY!? WHERE!? *(He consults pocket mirror, anxiously.)* Oh, you detestable child! Here's that for your 'satiable curtiosity! *(Gives him a smack and swishes off.)*

ELEPHANT. Well, gee whiz!

*(He pats his increasingly sore rump again. Enter* **HIPPO- POTAMUS**, *terribly hung over.)*

HIPPO. Oh, it's you, is it, Elephant's Child.

ELEPHANT. *(loudly and excitedly)* Good morning, Aunt Hippopotamus!

HIPPO. Sh-sh, please! Auntie has a headache.

**ELEPHANT.** A headache, Aunt Hippopotamus? Gee, that's too bad, can I rub your head for you, or how about an old banana skin to lay across your forehead, do you think that would make you feel better, how long has your head hurt you anyway, and what did you mean last night when you said you felt pickled, I thought only pickles could be pickled, and oh, gosh, Aunt Hippopotamus, what makes your eyes so red?

**HIPPO.** Oooh, my poor head! QUIET! Here's that for your 'satiable curtiosity! (*Another smack and she gropes her way offstage.*)

**ELEPHANT.** In trouble again. (*to audience*) Did you ever get into trouble for asking too many questions? Didn't it make you mad? Everybody says if you want to learn something you have to ask a question, and then you ask and they give you a swat instead of an answer! And I have so much that I wonder about. I wonder why they always think I'm naughty when all I want is just to understand! I wonder why they have to be so haughty And think they're just so absolutely grand! I wonder if my whole life is a blunder. I guess I'll never ever be a winner. And, oh, I've got another thing I wonder – What does the crocodile eat for his dinner?

**HIPPO, OSTRICH & GIRAFFE.** (*reentering*) HUSH!

**OSTRICH.** Here's a swat for always asking questions.

**HIPPO.** And here's a swat for making too much noise!

**GIRAFFE.** And here's a swat for always being pesty!

**ALL.** Now go and play with your expensive toys!

(*All stalk off.* **ELEPHANT** *is left crying. Enter the* **KOLO-KOLO BIRD**.)

**KOLO.** Hello, there, Elephant's child! What's the matter, no questions today?

**ELEPHANT.** Oh, hello, Kolokolo Bird.

**KOLO.** What's wrong, Elephant's Child?

**ELEPHANT.** My Aunt Ostrich spanked me, and my Aunt Hippopotamus spanked me, and my Uncle Giraffe spanked me. They all spanked me for my 'satiable curtiosity. And I still want to know what the crocodile has for dinner!

**KOLO.** Well, why don't you find out for yourself?

**ELEPHANT.** Find out for myself? How can I do that? I don't even know where the crocodile lives.

**KOLO.** It's time you saw a bit of the world, Elephant's Child. The Crocodile lives in the great, grey-green greasy Limpopo River.

**ELEPHANT.** The great, grey-green greasy Limpopo River? *(aside)* An answer! Somebody finally gave me an answer! But Kolokolo bird, what does the Crocodile look like?

**KOLO.** You must go to the banks of the great grey-green greasy Limpopo River, all set about with fever trees, and answer your own question.

**ELEPHANT.** *(with sudden determination)* Yes. I will. It is time I saw a bit of the world and found out some answers for myself. Thank you, Kolokolo Bird – I'm on my way. *(exits, singing, "Limpopo River, here I come!")*

**KOLO.** "What does the crocodile eat for dinner?" Oh, you'll find out, Elephant's Child, you'll find out! *(laughs through this speech, building to loud shrieks, exits at end)*

**ELEPHANT.** *(Re-enters. He is now on the banks of the Limpopo.)* I guess this is it – the great grey-green greasy Limpopo River. Yes – there are fever trees all right.

*(**PYTHON** enters and curls around a rock.)*

But where's the Crocodile? *(He sees the **PYTHON**.)* Oh! I wonder who that is! *(approaches)* Uh – sir? Ma'am? Who might you be?

**PYTHON.** I, my ignorant child? I am, of course, the Bi-Colored Python Rock-Snake. You, I presume, are an Elephant, or, at any rate, an Elephant's Child. Now kindly allow me to proceed with my slumbers.

**ELEPHANT.** 'Scuse me, but have you seen such a thing as a Crocodile in these promiscuous parts?

PYTHON. Have I seen a Crocodile? What will you think of next?

ELEPHANT. 'Scuse me, but could you kindly tell me what he has for dinner?

(**PYTHON** *uncurls his tail and quickly swats the* **ELEPHANT**.)

PYTHON. There! Now let me sleep!

ELEPHANT. That is odd. My Aunt Ostrich and Aunt Hippopotamus and Uncle Giraffe have all spanked me for my 'satiable curtiosity – and I suppose this is the very same thing. Well, goodbye, Bi-Colored Python Rock-Snake. Here, let me help you get comfortably coiled. There now. Don't mind me.

(*The* **CROCODILE** *enters, slithering through the water.*)

I'll just find the Crocodile all by myself. I'll just sit on this log and wait until one comes along.

(*He sits on the* **CROCODILE**.)

CROCODILE. (*Notices the* **ELEPHANT'S CHILD**, *looks up to him. Speaks with heavy irony.*) Quite comfy?

ELEPHANT. (*leaps up*) Oh! Why excuse me, but you see, I thought you were just an old log!

CROCODILE. Just an old log. I see. How flattering.

ELEPHANT. Uh-huh, but now I see you're not. Tell me, do you happen to have seen a crocodile in these promiscuous parts?

CROCODILE. (*moves toward* **ELEPHANT**) A crocodile? You're looking for a crocodile, are you?

(*He laughs loudly. The* **ELEPHANT** *moves away.*)

Come hither, little one. Why do you ask such things?

ELEPHANT. 'Scuse me, but were you going to spank me for my 'satiable curtiosity? You see, all my fearsome family have just spanked me, and the Bi-Colored Python Rock-Snake has just spanked me the hardest of all, with his scalesome flailsome tail! So if it's all the same to you, I'd rather not be spanked any more!

**CROCODILE.** Come hither, little one, for I am the Crocodile!

**ELEPHANT.** *(eagerly)* You're the Crocodile! *(suspiciously)* Prove it.

**CROCODILE.** Very well. *(He suddenly bursts into loud weeping, keeps it up for a moment, then stops just as suddenly.)* There. Crocodile tears. That's how you know.

**ELEPHANT.** *(impressed)* Oh, you really are the Crocodile, aren't you? You are the very person I have been looking for all these long days! Will you tell me please, what do you have for dinner?

**CROCODILE.** Come hither, little one, I'll whisper it to you.

*(The **ELEPHANT** approaches, gets his head close to the **CROCODILE'S** mouth.)*

I think – I think today I will begin with – the Elephant's Child!

*(He grabs the **ELEPHANT'S CHILD'**s nose between his teeth.)*

**ELEPHANT.** LED GO! YOU ARE HURTIG BE!

*(A great pulling begins. The **PYTHON** unfurls from the rock.)*

**PYTHON.** My young friend, if you do not now pull immediately and instantly, pull as hard as ever you can, it is my considered opinion that your large patent-leather acquaintance will jerk you into yonder stream before you can say Jack Robinson.

**ELEPHANT.** Huh?

**PYTHON.** Pull, you pitiful pachyderm, pull!

*(The pulling increases, and the nose of the **ELEPHANT** begins to stretch. The **CROCODILE** has the advantage.)*

**ELEPHANT.** This is too buch for be!

*(**PYTHON** slithers to **ELEPHANT'S CHILD** and wraps himself around his hind legs.)*

**PYTHON.** Now let us devote ourselves seriously to a little high tension before this armor plated submarine permanently sinks your battleship! *(aside)* That is the way all Bi-Colored Python Rock Snakes always talk.

*(A great pulling action ensues. The* **PYTHON** *and the* **ELEPHANT** *finally prevail. The* **CROCODILE** *falls into the water and the* **ELEPHANT'S CHILD** *falls back onto the* **PYTHON***.)*

**CROCODILE.** Curse you, Bi-Colored Python Rock Snake! I'll even the score one of these days! *(He slithers off.)*

**ELEPHANT.** Oh, thank you, Bi-Colored Python Rock Snake! Python? Oh, there you are! *(He gets up.)* But oh, my poor, poor nose! *(He dips it into the Limpopo.)*

**PYTHON.** Just what do you think you're doing?

**ELEPHANT.** 'Scuse me, but my nose is badly out of shape, and I am waiting for it to shrink.

**PYTHON.** Then you will have to wait a long time. Some people don't know what's good for them.

**ELEPHANT.** You mean it'll never be the same again? I'll have to go through my whole life with this – this – huge thing? Why it's big enough to pack all my clothes in! It's like a suitcase – uh, a briefcase – uh…

**PYTHON.** Trunk?

**ELEPHANT.** That's it! A trunk!

**PYTHON.** *(aside)* I always did have a way with words.

**ELEPHANT.** Oh, but what will I do with a trunk? *(He discovers a fly on his shoulder and absently flicks it off, with his trunk, of course.)*

**PYTHON.** Vantage number one! You couldn't have done that with a mere smear nose. Don't you think it's warm?

*(Impulsively, the* **ELEPHANT** *dips his trunk into the river and gives himself a shower bath. He is delighted with his newfound ability.)*

Vantage number two! You couldn't have done that with a mere smear nose! Now how do you feel about being spanked again?

**ELEPHANT.** 'Scuse me, but I should not like it at all!

**PYTHON.** Well, if I am correct, I see your regrettable relatives off yonder, and they seem to be progressing in our direction. No doubt they are searching for you. Perhaps you will find another use for your trunk on this occasion!

*(The Relatives enter, both relieved and angry.)*

**OSTRICH.** So there you are at last, you naughty child! How dare you wander so far from home! We've been worried sick! Come here and be spanked for your 'satiable curtiosity!

**ELEPHANT.** Ha! I don't think you peoples know anything about spanking, but I do, and I'll show you!

*(He gives **OSTRICH** a whack on the behind with his trunk. It knocks her head-first into the sand.)*

**HIPPO.** Oh, bananas! Where did you learn that trick, and what have you done to your nose?

**ELEPHANT.** *(As he answers, he is chasing and swatting Aunt **HIPPO**.)* I got a new one from the Crocodile! *(swat)* I asked him what he had for dinner *(swat)* and he gave me this to keep! *(swat)*

*(Aunt **HIPPO** retires.)*

**GIRAFFE.** Well, it's very useful but it looks very ugly!

*(**ELEPHANT** grabs one of uncle **GIRAFFE'S** legs and hurls him into a hornet's nest.)*

Hornets! Hornets! Yowie! *(He runs off, yelling.)*

**PYTHON.** Didn't I say, Elephant's Child, that you would find a use for your trunk?

**ELEPHANT.** Oh, thank you, Python, dear friend! I've never felt so strong! So powerful! They'd better respect me now! *(He tastes one moment of utter glory.)* But gee, do you think I was a little rough on them? I guess they were really worried about me, huh? Maybe I'd better go and see. Oh, Aunt Hippo! Aunt Ostrich! Are you all right? *(He runs off.)*

**PYTHON.** There he goes – as strong as a hundred men now, but still a curious child at heart. Noses may change, but natures don't. How true, how true.

*(He composes himself for sleep, still chatting away to the audience, as the* **CROCODILE** *slips back onstage, takes him by the tail, and slowly pulls him off.)*

He would never have made the adjustment without me. Matter of fact, he would never have freed himself from the Crocodile's clutches without me. Brains. That's what I have. Brains. You have to be clever in this world. You can't let the next fellow put one over on you. *(He is off.)*

### "FIRST SING-SONG OF OLD MAN KANGAROO"

*(The* **KANGAROO** *segments are spoken chants. They are strongly accentuated and rhythmically varied. The actors should find the natural rhythms and forward motion of the piece without becoming too sing-song. It is a delicate balance. Lines may be reassigned among the actors to suit the choreography.)*

**KANGAROO.** Not always was the kangaroo as now we do behold him. *(***KANGAROO** *displays his usual self.)*

**ACTOR #2.** But a different animal –

**ACTOR #3.** With four short legs

**ALL.** Short legs, short legs, short legs, hah!

*(***KANGAROO** *squats to show four short legs.)*

**ACTOR #4.** He was grey –

**ACTOR #5.** And he was woolly –

**ACTOR #3.** And his pride was inordinate –

*(***KANGAROO** *shows inordinate pride.)*

**ACTOR #6.** He danced on an outcrop in the middle of Australia –

**ACTORS #2, 3, 6.** And he went to the Little God Nqa.

**KANGAROO.** Little God Nqa?

**NQA.** Who is disturbing me?

**KANGAROO.** Little God, Little God –

**NQA.** It's 6 a.m.!

**KANGAROO.** Make me special…make me better…Make me different from all the other animals – by five this afternoon!

**NQA.** Make you special? Make you better? Make you different? Go away!

**ACTOR #3.** He was grey –

**ACTOR #5.** And he was wooly –

**ACTOR #3.** And his pride was inordinate!

**ACTOR #2.** He danced on a sandbank in the middle of Australia

**ACTORS #3, 6.** And he went to the Middle God Nquing.

**KANGAROO.** Middle God Nquing?

**NQUING.** What do you want with me?

**KANGAROO.** Middle God, Middle God –

**NQUING.** My breakfast's hot!

**KANGAROO.** Make me special…make me popular…Make me better than all the other animals by five this afternoon!

**NQUING.** Make you special? Make you better? Make you popular? Go away!

**ACTOR #2.** He was grey –

**ACTOR #5.** And he was woolly –

**ACTOR #3.** And his pride was –

**ALL.** INORDINATE!

**ACTOR #2.** He danced on an ashpit in the middle of Australia

**ACTORS #2, 3, 4, 5.** And he went to the Big God Nquong.

**KANGAROO.** Big God Nquong?

**NQUONG.** Who is addressing me?

**KANGAROO.** Big God, Big God –

**NQUONG.** You, watch your step!

**KANGAROO.** Make me better…make me different…Make me popular and wonder-fly run after by five this afternoon!

NQUONG. Make you different? Make you popular? Make you run after? Yes, I will! Dingo! Dingo! Yellow dog Dingo! Always hungry Dingo, sleeping in the sun! Dingo! Dingo! Wake up, Dingo! Do you see that gentleman dancing on the ashpit?

DINGO. What, that cat-rabbit?

NQUONG. Yep, that's him. He wants to be popular, And very much run after, Dingo, make him go!

ACTOR #5. Up jumped Dingo, yellow dog Dingo.

ACTOR #3. Always hungry Dingo

ACTOR #4. Up he jumped –

ALL. And grinned at Kangaroooooo….

ACTOR #5. Off went the proud Kangaroo

ACTOR #3. Like a bunny –

ACTOR #4. Like a bunny on his four little legs

ACTOR #3. Like a bunny – -

ACTOR #5. And the yellow dog Dingo –

ACTOR #4. Always hungry Dingo –

ACTOR #2. Grinning like a Jack-o-lantern

ALL. Flew after Kangaroo, phew!

ACTOR #5. And this ends the first part –

ACTOR #3. Of –

ACTOR #4. The –

ACTOR #2. Tale!

### *HUMP SAYS THE CAMEL. – PART TWO*

*(Break from Kangaroo sing-song.* CAMEL *enters, looks everyone over, gives a couple of humphs, crosses to exit, turns back, and humphs again.)*

ACTOR #3. Oh, it's you again. Come here, Camel.

CAMEL. Humph!

ACTOR #2. Listen, instead of just sneering you could help out.

ACTOR #3. Yes! What about joining us?

ACTOR #4. You could help out with costumes.

**ACTOR #5.** Or move scenery – it's heavy, you know.

**ACTOR #1.** Or listen – maybe you could even learn a part. Let's hear you say something.

**CAMEL.** Humph!

**ACTOR #3.** Besides humph! I mean, this is a high class organization. Were're used to a little more enthusiasm, buster!

**CAMEL.** *(One more elegant sneer and he's gone.)* HIP, HIP, HUMPH.

**ACTOR #1.** Ooh, he makes me so mad!

**ACTOR #2.** *(restrains* **ACTOR #1** *from rushing off and hitting* **CAMEL***)* No, let him go. He's just a howler.

**ACTOR #1.** But all he does is make fun of everyone else! I'll give him such a smack! *(has to be restrained again)*

**ACTOR #3.** Oh, he'll get his some day. Him and his "humph."

*(They exit.* **PARSEE** *enters and takes center stage.)*

### *"HOW THE RHINOCEROS GOT HIS SKIN"*

**PARSEE.** Once upon a time, on an island on the shores of the Red Sea, there lived a Parsee. Ahem…my humble self. My name is Pestonjee Bomonjee, and from my hat, the rays of the sun are reflected in more than oriental splendor! *(He does a bit with his hat, puts it on, preens a bit.)* And the Parsee – my humble self – lived by the Red Sea with nothing but a hat, a knife, and a cooking stove. I do love to cook! I think I'll bake a cake.

FLOUR AND WATER, CURRANTS AND PLUMS,

SUGAR AND THINGS, MIX IT WITH YOUR THUMBS,

BAKE IT IN THE OVEN,

THEN EAT IT QUICK! OR AS QUICK AS YOU CAN,

CAUSE IT'S TWO FEET ACROSS

AND TWO FEET THICK! JUST THE SIZE FOR A MAN.

Sniff, mmm, a superior comestible. Sniff, sniff, mmm, mmm! It smells *most* sentimental!

*(Opens mouth and prepares to eat. He freezes mid-action as the* **RHINOCEROS** *snorts his way onto the stage.)*

**RHINO.** Strorks! Snort, snort.

**PARSEE.** Why good morning to you, Mr. Rhinoceros.

**RHINO.** Cake!

**PARSEE.** Cake? Cake? Where? *(Looks around, then pretends to be surprised to find that he's holding it.)* Oh, you mean this cake! Yes, it certainly is, isn't it? *(sniffs)* I don't think it's much good, though. Stale, don't you know. I really think…

**RHINO.** CAKE!

**PARSEE.** Why, Mr. Rhinoceros – if you have cake at this hour, you'll spoil your dinner. How many times has your mother said to you –

**RHINO.** I'm sooo hungry! *(snort snort)*

**PARSEE.** But you'll get pimples if you eat too many sweets! Pimples all over your nice smooth skin.

**RHINO.** It is nice and smooth, isn't it?

**PARSEE.** Lovely. Really lovely. A beautiful tight fit. No wrinkles anywhere.

**RHINO.** I know.

*(Contemplates himself lovingly for a moment and* **PARSEE** *takes advantage by trying to slip away with his cake.* **RHINO** *snaps out of it, catching* **PARSEE** *in mid-sneak.)*

Oh, Parsee, couldn't I have just a little piece?

**PARSEE.** *(all innocence)* Piece of what?

**RHINO.** Cake! CAKE!

**PARSEE.** Well, very well.

**PARSEE.** *(With extreme reluctance, he breaks off a small piece and hands it to* **RHINO**.*)* There.

**RHINO.** *(snarfs it up immediately)* Yum. More! More!

**PARSEE.** But this is my cake! I baked it. It's *mine!*

**RHINO.** Just one more piece, please?

**PARSEE.** Oh, all right. But this is it!

*(Same business. **PARSEE** breaks off a small piece, **RHINO** gobbles it up.)*

**PARSEE.** There now. Was that good?

**RHINO.** *(simply)* Yes. Now I want it *all*!

**PARSEE.** Oh no! I told you that was it. You've had the *it* one.

**RHINO.** *(suddenly ferocious)* I want it all!

**PARSEE.** *(frightened)* But Rhinoceros, remember your complexion, what a nice smooth skin you have!

**RHINO.** Strorks! *(snort, snort)*

**PARSEE.** Why Rhinoceros, what little piggy eyes you have!

*(**RHINO** snorts, licks his chops and moves toward the cake.)*

Why, Rhinoceros, what a big horn you have on your nose!

*(**PARSEE** runs for the nearest tree and climbs it. **RHINO** eats the cake, piggishly, with much smacking and snorting. Then he looks around inside stove to find more, and upsets the stove.)*

*(furiously, from the tree)* You have no manners, you never did have any manners, and you never will have any manners!

*(**PARSEE** throws his hat at the **RHINO** in a fury. **RHINO** dodges, then looks disdainfully at **PARSEE**.)*

**RHINO.** Strorks. *(He waddles over to hat and deliberately steps on it. Then he sashays off.)*

**PARSEE.** *(Coming down from tree, muttering in unintelligible fury…First he rescues hat, then he picks up stove.)*

Them that takes cakes

Which the Parsee-man bakes

Makes dreadful mistakes.

Five weeks later there was a heat wave at the Red Sea, and everybody took off all the clothes they had and went to the beach for a swim. *(mime walk to beach)* Too darn hot for this hat!

(**PARSEE** *takes it off, lays it ceremoniously aside, then mimes entering water, splashing himself joyously and swimming away.*)

**RHINO.** *(entering)* Too darn hot for this skin!

(*He takes off "skin" – coat, jacket, or whatever – lays it down carelessly and waddles into the water, snorts, blows bubbles, and swims away.* **PARSEE** *re-enters, climbs out of water, shakes himself off. As he reaches for his hat, he notices the skin.*)

**PARSEE.** Hello, what's this? Somebody down with the heat? I say, old chap, buck up – why – it's just a skin – a nice smooth skin…it looks…it looks just like…
*(to audience)*
Did you happen to see who left this skin here?
*(audience answers)*
I knew it! AHA!

(*The* **PARSEE** *smiles, then laughs, building to maniacal glee. He dances three times round the skin, rubbing his hands, miming actions to the following words.*)

I think I'll just take a quick run back to my camp and see what I can find in my oven…Ah, yes! It's just filled with old, stale, leftover crumbs.
*(He gleefully fills his hat with crumbs.)*
I love a good crumb cake, don't you? Now, back to the beach! Aha! Still here! Now, Mr. Rude, Mr. No-manners, never-will-have-any-manners, we'll just see!
*(miming gestures again)*
I'm gonna *take* that skin
And *shake* that skin
And *scrub* that skin
And *rub* that skin
Just full of old, dry, stale, *(wow!)* tickly crumbs!

(**PARSEE** *makes big production out of scrunching crumbs all over inside of skin. Speaks to an audience member.*)

You wanna help? Come up here!

*(Child comes onstage.)*

We're gonna TAKE that skin
and SHAKE that skin
and SCRUB that skin
and RUB that skin
Just full of old, dry, stale, tickly crumbs!
Ah! Superior. Superior. Now you go back to your seat and I will climb to the top of this palm tree and we'll all wait for Mr. No-Manners to come put his skin back on.

*(He climbs.* **RHINO** *enters from the water, snorts prodigiously and shakes himself off. Then he puts his skin back on, looks down with satisfaction at how nice and smooth it is. A beat. He finds a tiny itch. Scratches it. Another. Then another. More and more itches make themselves felt. Finally it itches him like crazy. He addresses audience.)*

**RHINO.** Who's a good back scratcher? You? Come up here! Can you help me with a little itch on my back? Just scratch, right here. No, higher, higher…to the right… up – no, down, down, ooh, you're not getting it!

*(***RHINO*** flops down, rubbing his back on the sand, rolling and rolling and itching worse and worse.)*

Oooh, it's all over! Worse and worse! *(gets up)* The palm tree has a nice rough bark. I'll try that. *(He runs to tree, rubs against it, pushing his skin into folds.)*

**PARSEE.** Why Mr. No-Manners, what a lumpy, bumpy, scaliferous skin you have!

*(***RHINO*** stops, looks, bellows in fury, stumps off, snorting and scratching. ***PARSEE*** climbs down.)*

And from that day to this, every rhinoceros has great folds in his skin and a very bad temper, all on account of the cake crumbs inside.

*(***PARSEE*** carefully cleans out the inside of his hat, puts it on, smiles hugely at audience.)*

Them that takes cakes
Which the Parsee man bakes
Makes dreadful mistakes!

### *"THE BEGINNING OF ARMADILLOS"*

**MOTHER.** *(to audience, very graciously)* Hello there, darlings, hello. You may not know it, but I am a jaguar, one of the fastest, and of course most beautiful, of the big jungle cats. But enough about me. A mother doesn't need the spotlight. I really want you to meet my little girl. Doffles, come here!

**DOFFLES.** *(bounds in)* Here I am, Ma!

**MOTHER.** Ah, yes, dear. Now, I want you to show all these lovely people how clever you are! Let's do our latest lesson for them.

**DOFFLES.** *(embarrassed)* Oh, Ma!

**MOTHER.** Come now dear. Ready? Now. When you find a stickly-prickly porcupine…

(**PORCUPINE** *enters, signifies to audience that that's him.*)

**DOFFLES.** When you find a porky-pine…

**MOTHER.** You must…you must… *(She mimes to help daughter get the answer.)*

**DOFFLES.** Drop him in the water and then he will…

(**MOTHER** *mimes uncoiling.*)

Uncoil!

(**PORCUPINE** *looks horrified.*)

**MOTHER.** Right darling! And when you catch a slow-solid tortoise…

(**TORTOISE** *enters in time to catch his own name and identify himself to audience.*)

**DOFFLES.** When I catch a tortoise?

**MOTHER.** You remember, darling, when you catch a tortoise… *(She mimes action of scooping to prompt her again.)*

**DOFFLES.** You must scoop him out of his shell with your paw.

*(TORTOISE looks horrified.)*

**MOTHER.** Splendid darling! *(to audience)* Isn't she the cleverest little thing? Now, Doffles, Mother is going to leave you on your own to see how well you can do. I'll be back. Now, be a good little jaguar and remember your lessons. *(to audience)* Isn't she precious? *(She exits.)*

**DOFFLES.** Ha! On my own at last! I'm the toughest little jaguar in this whole jungle! And I'm fast!

*(She spots the **PORCUPINE** and **TORTOISE,** who are slowly trying to creep away.)*

I'm real fast!

*(She pounces and lands before them, cutting off their exit.)*

Ha! Caught you both! Now come here!

*(She drags them both center, one on either side. They both assume defensive positions, the **PORCUPINE** curled into a ball and the **TORTOISE** withdrawn into his shell.)*

Ha! I've caught a Porky-pine! And a Tortoise! Or is it a Tortoise and a Porky-pine? Now which is which?

*(She taps them both sharply on the back.)*

Now listen here, fellows. This is very important! My mother said that when I meet a Porkypine I am to drop him into the water to make him uncoil, and when I meet a Tortoise I am to scoop him out of his shell with my paw. Now which one is Porkypine and which one is Tortoise? Because, to save my spots, I can't tell!

**PORCUPINE.** Are you sure of what your Mommy told you? Are you quite sure? Perhaps she said that when you uncoil a Tortoise you must shell him out of the water with a scoop and when you paw a Porcupine you must drop him on the shell!

**TORTOISE.** Or maybe she said that when you water a Porcupine you must drop him into your paw and when you meet a Tortoise you must shell him until he uncoils!

**DOFFLES.** Now, wait a minute –

**PORCUPINE.** When you scoop water with your paw you uncoil it with a Porcupine. Remember that because it's important!

**TORTOISE.** But, when you paw your meat, you must drop it into a Tortoise with a scoop. Why can't you understand?

**DOFFLES.** Stop, stop! I don't want your advice! I only want to know which of you is Porky-pine and which one is Tortoise!

**PORCUPINE.** I won't tell you. But you can scoop me out of my shell if you like.

**DOFFLES.** Aha! Now I know you're the Tortoise! You thought I wouldn't! Now I will.

(**DOFFLES** *swipes with her paw just as* **PORCUPINE** *curls into a ball. She gets a pawful of prickles. And the* **PORCUPINE** *rolls offstage.*)

**DOFFLES.** *(cont.)* Ow! Prickles! Ow! Owowowowow!

(*She dances about, shaking her paw, puts it into her mouth, hurts her mouth, yells again. Finally calms down.*)

Why, he wasn't a Tortoise at all! But how do I know that this other one is Tortoise?

**TORTOISE.** But I am Tortoise! Your mother was quite right. She said that you were to scoop me out of my shell with your paw. Begin.

**DOFFLES.** You didn't say that a minute ago. You said something different.

**TORTOISE.** Well, just because you say that I said that she said something different, what difference does that make? Because if she said what you said I said she said, it's just the same as if I said what she said she said. On the other hand, if you think she said to uncoil me with a scoop, and not to paw me into drops with a shell, it isn't my fault!

**DOFFLES.** I don't believe you. You've mixed up all the things my mother said with all the things you asked me if I was sure she didn't say and I'm so confused! Now let me think. Hmmm. My mother told me that I was to drop one of you in the water. And you seem so anxious to be uncoiled that I think you really don't want to be dropped! Ok...you jump into that water.

**TORTOISE.** All right, but when your mother doesn't like it, don't blame me! (**TORTOISE** *jumps in water and swims away.*)

**DOFFLES.** (*Looks after* **TORTOISE** *in disbelief. Looks in direction of* **PORCUPINE.** *Sucks her paw.*) Ma? Ma?! MAAA!

**MOTHER.** (*entering*) Darling, darling! What have you been doing that you shouldn't have done?

**DOFFLES.** I tried to scoop out something that said it wanted to be scooped out of its shell with my paw and my paw is full of per-ickles!

**MOTHER.** Darling. That must have been a Porcupine! You should have dropped him in the water.

**DOFFLES.** I did that to the other thing, and he said he was a Tortoise and I didn't believe him and it was quite true and he dived in and swam away and I haven't had anything to eat all day-ay-ay! (*Ends on a wail.*)

**MOTHER.** Darling. Now listen and remember what I say:

(**PORCUPINE** *and* **TORTOISE** *enter and listen, unseen.*)

A Porcupine curls himself into a ball and his prickles stick out every which way at once. By this you may know the Porcupine.

(**TORTOISE** *joins* **PORCUPINE.**)

**PORCUPINE.** I don't like this old lady one bit. I wonder what else she knows?

**MOTHER.** A Tortoise can't curl himself up. He only draws his head and legs into his shell. By this you may know the Tortoise.

**TORTOISE.** I don't like this old lady at all…at all! Even Doffles can't forget those directions. It's too bad you can't swim, stickly-prickly.

**PORCUPINE.** Don't talk to me! Just think how much better it would be if you could curl up. This is a mess! Just listen to the Jaguar.

**DOFFLES.** Can't curl, but can swim – slow-solid, that's him! Curls up, but can't swim – stickly-prickly, that's him!

**MOTHER.** That's right dear. You just keep saying that, and we'll put a bandaid on your poor little paddy-paw.

*(She leads her off,* **DOFFLES** *repeating her lesson.)*

**PORCUPINE.** She'll never forget that in a month of Sundays! What'll we do?

**TORTOISE.** I don't know, partner. Looks like it's sink or swim.

**PORCUPINE.** Tortoise, I think you've got the answer! I'll just have to learn to swim!

**TORTOISE.** But I was just joking

**PORCUPINE.** Well, I'm not! *(to audience)* I need two people to teach me to swim. Who can help?

*(Volunteers are selected:* **PORCUPINE** *works improvisationally with children, helped by* **TORTOISE***. First he gets them to demonstrate in mime. Then he tries and sinks a couple of times, elicits their advice about what he's doing wrong, and finally, triumphantly, learns to swim.)*

I think I've got it! Yes, I've got it! I can swim! Thank you! Let's have some applause for my helpers! You can go back to your seats now.

**TORTOISE.** Oh, thank you, thank you…But what about me? Now you can swim but I can't…say…maybe if I had helpers I could learn to coil up into a ball! *(to audience)* Could two more of you come up and help me?

*(Two more volunteers are selected.* **TORTOISE** *works improvisationally with them, helped by the* **PORCUPINE***. He gets them to loosen his shell and roll him into a ball. He's very stiff at first and complains of pain but finally is victorious.)*

**TORTOISE.** Now I can do it too! I can roll into a ball! Oh, thank you. Thank you! Let's have a big round of applause for my helpers!

*(He sends them back to their seats.)*

**PORCUPINE.** Well, look at you, Tortoise! I wouldn't know you from my own family! Your shell has stretched out into scales. Just try not to grunt so much when you curl up!

**TORTOISE.** I'll try. Why, Porcupine, your prickles seem to have melted into each other. Your back looks like a hard pine-cone!

**PORCUPINE.** Really? It must be from soaking in the water and then baking in the sun.

**TORTOISE.** Actually, we look very much alike now!

**PORCUPINE.** Yes, we do, don't we? Oh, here comes the little jaguar. Won't she be confused!

**DOFFLES.** *(entering)* "Can't curl, but can swim, slow-solid, that's him."

**PORCUPINE.** Good morning! And how is your dear gracious little mommy this morning?

**DOFFLES.** She is fine, but who are you?

**PORCUPINE.** Who am I? But don't you remember me? After all, just yesterday you tried to scoop me out of my shell!

**DOFFLES.** But you hadn't any shell! It was all prickles! I know it was. Just look at my paw!

**TORTOISE.** You told me to jump in the river and drown. Why are you so rude and forgetful today?

**PORCUPINE.** Don't you remember what your mother told you? "Can't curl, but can swim, Stickly-Prickly, that's him! Curls up but can't swim, Slow-solid, that's him!"

*(**PORCUPINE** and **TORTOISE** both take a swim, then curl up and roll around and around.)*

**DOFFLES.** Ma? Ma!? Maaa!

**MOTHER.** *(entering)* Darling, what's the matter now?

**DOFFLES.** Ma, there's two new animals in the woods today, and the one you said couldn't swim swims and the one you said couldn't curl curls. And they're both scaly, instead of one being smooth and one being prickly. And besides that they're rolling around and around in circles and I don't feel comfy!

**MOTHER.** Darling, a Porcupine is a Porcupine and can't be anything but a Porcupine, and a Tortoise is a Tortoise and can never be anything else.

**DOFFLES.** But – they aren't Porkypines and they aren't Tortoises. They're a little bit of both and I don't know their proper names.

**MOTHER.** Nonsense! Everything has its proper name. I should call them…"Armadillos." And I should leave them alone. Come along, dear. *(They exit.)*

**PORCUPINE.** "I should call them Armadillos!"

**TORTOISE.** "And I should leave them alone!" *(They laugh.)*

**PORCUPINE.** Well, friend, separately we may have our faults…

**TORTOISE.** But together we're perfection!

### *"SECOND SING-SONG OF OLD MAN KANGAROO"*

**ACTOR #2.** Who is coming, who?

**ACTOR #3.** Old man Kangaroo!

**ACTOR #5.** Running through the desert and the mountains and the salt pans

**ALL.** Running

**ACTOR #4.** Running through the reed beds

**ALL.** Running

**ACTOR #3.** Running through the spinifex!

**ALL.** He has to!

**ACTOR #2.** Old man Kangaroo! Who is after you?

**KANGAROO.** *(Retard the rhythm, then build intensity, legato.)*
Dingo, Dingo, yellow Dingo,
Grinning like a rat-trap, Dingo

**DINGO.** Never getting nearer, never,
Never getting farther, either,

**KANGAROO & DINGO.** After Kangaroo!

**ACTORS #3 & #5.** Kangaroo and Dingo, running through the ti-trees;

**ACTOR #4.** mulga

**ACTOR #3.** short grass

**ACTOR #5.** long grass

**ALL.** Running

**ACTOR #2.** Running through the tropics of Capricorn and Cancer

**ALL.** And right to the Wallgong River!

**ACTOR #2.** The Wallgong River where there isn't any bridge!

**ACTOR #5.** The Wallgong River where there isn't any ferry boat!

**ACTOR #3.** And here comes Dingo

**ACTOR #4.** Yellow dog Dingo

**ACTOR #2.** Now he's getting nearer

**ACTOR #5.** Grinning like a horse-collar

**ALL.** What will Kangaroo do?

**ACTOR #2.** Well, that ends the second part

**ACTOR #5.** Of –

**ACTOR #4.** our –

**ACTOR #3.** tale!

### HUMP SAYS THE CAMEL – PART THREE

*(Actors break from kangaroo sing-song. Same business:* **CAMEL** *enters, does his "humph" routine and exits, leaving fury in his wake.)*

**ACTOR #4.** *What* can we do about the Camel? He's spoiling everything!

**ACTOR #6.** Him and his Humph!, I'd like to humph him!

**ACTOR #4.** Say – who's that rolling along in a cloud of dust?

**DJINNI.** *(leaps onstage)* It is I – the Djinni of all Deserts! I always travel along in a cloud of dust because it is magic! *(He slaps himself, and clouds of dust roll off him.)*

Down! Down, Lawrence!

**ACTOR #4.** Djinni of all Deserts – is it right for anyone to make fun of everybody else all the time?

**DJINNI.** Certainly not.

**ACTOR #6.** Well, there's a thing in the middle of your Howling desert...

**ACTOR #4.** ...and he's a Howler himself!

**ACTOR #6.** ...with a long neck and long legs and all he says is humph!

**DJINNI.** Ha! That's my Camel, for all the gold in Arabia! Does he say anything else?

**ACTOR #4.** Only Humph! And all he does is sneer.

**DJINNI.** Very well. The next time he appears I shall take matters into my own hands. But meanwhile *(grandly)* on with the show!

### *"THE CAT THAT WALKS BY HIMSELF"*

**ACTOR #3.** Long, long ago, Best Beloved, the whole world was wild. The Dog was wild... *(becomes* **DOG***)*

**ACTOR #2.** And the Horse was wild *(becomes* **HORSE***)*

**ACTOR #3.** And the Cow was wild... *(becomes* **COW***, giving a profound moo)* Well, as wild as a cow could be. And they walked in the Wet Wild Woods by their wild selves.

**ACTOR #4.** But the wildest of all the wild animals was the Cat. *(becomes cat)* He walked by himself, and all places were alike to him.

**ACTOR #5.** Of course the Man was wild too. He was dreadfully wild.

*(He breaks into a wild, hooting, hollering dance. The animals scatter.)*

**ACTOR #6. (WOMAN)** He didn't even begin to be tame until he met – the Woman.

*(***WOMAN*** strikes a sexy pose. ***MAN*** sees her, stops dancing, stands stupidly and looks at her in dumb admiration. She undulates over to him. Sweetly.)*

I do not like living in your wild ways.

*(She socks him a good one on the jaw and he falls.
Briskly)*

**WOMAN.** *(cont.)* Now then. We need a nice dry cave to live
in, not that pile of wet leaves you have. *(establishes cave
space)* I'll just light a fire under my stew pot *(miming
actions)* and put some sweet fresh hay on the floor, and
a nice fur rug on the hearth. Wipe your feet, dear,
when you come in, and now we'll keep house.

**MAN.** *(enters slowly, sniffing the stew)* Um. Yum.

**WOMAN.** *(continuously bustling as she serves dinner)* Dinner
tonight is wild sheep made with wild garlic and wild
pepper, wild duck stuffed with wild rice and wild
fenugreek and wild coriander, and marrow bones
of wild oxen, and for dessert, wild cherries and wild
grenadillas.

*(He eats, hungrily and sloppily. She produces a napkin
and tucks it around his neck.)*

Now wipe your wild, wild chin.

*(The **MAN** yawns, stretches out before the fire and dozes
off. The **WOMAN** begins to comb out her hair, humming
a song. Lights cross-fade to focus on the animals who
have gathered on the other side of the stage.)*

**HORSE.** Oh my friends, why have the Man and the Woman
made that great light in the great cave?

**COW.** Will it do us any harm?

**CAT.** *(yawns unconcernedly)* What has it to do with us?

**DOG.** *(sniffing the food smells)* Maybe everything. It smells
good to me! I will go and look.

**HORSE.** Be careful, Dog! Man is wild and treacherous.

**DOG.** Come with me then, Horse. Two can be braver than
one.

**HORSE.** Very well. Cow, come along. Three can be braver
than two.

**COW.** Oh, all right. Cat, you'd better come too. Four can
be braver than three.

**CAT.** Oh, no.

**DOG.** Please come, Cat. Friends should walk together in this wild, wild world.

**CAT.** Foolish Dog, I always walk alone. I am the Cat who walks by himself, and all places are alike to me.

**DOG.** But I thought you were my friend.

*(Pause. **CAT** turns away.)*

We can never be friends again.

*(**CAT** shrugs, starts to wash his face.)*

Forget him. Follow me.

*(The animals move quietly toward the cave. As soon as the **CAT** is left alone, he stops washing his face and looks after the other animals.)*

**CAT.** Since all places are alike to me, I will go and see too. But alone.

*(He follows the other animals, unnoticed by them. Lights cross fade to cave area.)*

**DOG.** You wait here. *(sniffing hungrily)* I will go first.

*(**HORSE** and **COW** withdraw upstage of cave. **CAT** hides and eavesdrops. **WOMAN** notices the **DOG** waiting at the cave entrance and laughs.)*

**WOMAN.** Here comes the first. Wild thing out of the Wild Woods, what do you want?

**DOG.** Oh my Enemy, what is it that smells so good?

**WOMAN.** *(picks up bone)* Try this bone, wild thing – taste, and you'll see.

*(She throws dog the bone. He chews it and loves it.)*

**DOG.** Oh my Enemy, give me another!

**WOMAN.** Wild thing out of the Wild Woods, help my Man to hunt through the day and guard this cave at night, and I will give you all the roast bones you need.

**CAT.** Ah! That is a very wise woman, but she is not so wise as I am.

**DOG.** *(enters cave and puts his head on the* **WOMAN'S** *lap)* Oh my Friend, I will help your Man to hunt through the day, and at night I will guard your cave.

*(**DOG** snuggles down to sleep. **WOMAN** pats his head and hums. **HORSE** moves hesitantly to the cave entrance.)*

**WOMAN.** *(notices* **HORSE** *and laughs)* Here comes the second.

*(**COW** moves to join **HORSE**.)*

And the third. Wild things out of the wild woods, what do you want?

**HORSE.** Oh my Enemy, we have come in search of Wild Dog.

*(**HORSE** sniffs the grass on the floor. So does **COW**. **WOMAN** laughs.)*

**WOMAN.** Wild thing out of the Wild Woods, you did not come here for Wild Dog, but for the sake of the sweet, fresh hay on my floor.

**HORSE.** True.

**COW.** Please give us some to eat.

**WOMAN.** Bend your head, Wild Horse.

*(She takes off her tie belt and slips it over* **HORSE'S** *neck.)*

Wear this and carry my Man on your back, and you will eat the sweet, fresh hay three times a day.

**HORSE.** Oh my mistress, I will be your servant for the sake of the sweet, fresh hay.

**CAT.** What a foolish Horse.

**COW.** And I?

**WOMAN.** If you will give me your warm white milk every day, you too may eat the sweet, fresh hay.

**COW.** Oh my Mistress, I will be your servant for the sake of the sweet, fresh hay.

**CAT.** What a foolish Cow.

*(**HORSE** and **COW** are given large bundles of hay to eat by the **WOMAN**. **MAN** wakes up. The first thing he sees is **WILD DOG** sleeping beside him. He leaps to his feet,*

*waking the* **DOG** *and generally stirring everyone up, except for the* **WOMAN**.*)*

**MAN.** Ho! Ha! Help! What is Wild Dog doing in here?

**WOMAN.** His name is not Wild Dog any more, but the First Friend, because he will be be our friend for always and always. Take him with you when you go hunting.

**MAN.** Hunting. Hunting. Where is my spear?

*(He looks around and walks smack into* **HORSE**, *who whinnies loudly.)*

Ha! Help! Help! What is Wild Horse doing in here?

**WOMAN.** His name is not Wild Horse any more, but the First Servant, because he will carry us from place to place for always and always. Ride on his back when you go hunting.

**MAN.** Yes. Hunting. Hunting. Where did you say you put my spear?

*(***COW** *stirs, moos loudly and walks to center of cave, waiting to be milked. The* **MAN** *takes this in, then purposefully crosses to the* **WOMAN**. *Confidentially)*

What is Wild Cow doing in here?

**WOMAN.** Her name is not Wild Cow any more, but the Giver of Good Food. She will give us the warm white milk for always and always while you and the First Friend and the First Servant go hunting.

*(As* **MAN** *turns automatically to start the spear search again,* **WOMAN** *kindly but firmly hands it to him.* **MAN** *tentatively pats* **DOG** *on head, then mounts the* **HORSE** *rather gingerly, gets on backwards, realizes that won't work, mounts properly. He decides that he is pleased with the arrangement, and charges off.)*

**MAN.** Ya-Ma-Ha! *(His war cry)*

*(***MAN**, **HORSE**, **DOG** *exit.* **WOMAN** *sits down to milk the* **COW**.*)*

**CAT.** Ah, this is a clever Woman, but she is not so clever as I am. *(smells the milk and approaches the cave entrance)* Meow. *(sits fetchingly at the doorway)*

**WOMAN**. And who might you be?

> (**CAT** *meows pitifully, does a routine suggesting that hunger is acute and death is imminent unless milk is served immediately.* **WOMAN** *laughs.*)

**WOMAN**. *(cont.)* Wild thing out of the Wild Woods, go back to the Wild Woods. We need no more friends or servants in our Cave.

**CAT**. I am not a Friend, and I am not a Servant. I am the Cat who walks by himself, and I wish to come into your Cave.

**WOMAN**. Then why didn't you come with the Others?

**CAT**. *(angry)* Has Wild Dog told tales of me?

**WOMAN**. *(amused)* You are the Cat who walks by himself, and all places are alike to you. You are neither a Friend nor a servant. You said so yourself. Go away and walk by yourself, then.

**CAT**. *(pretending to be sorry)* Can't I ever come into the Cave? Can't I ever sit by the fire and drink the warm white milk? How can you be so cruel to a poor little hungry Cat? You can't – I know you can't. You're too wise – you're too beautiful.

**WOMAN**. *(flattered)* Beautiful. Oh. I knew I was wise, but I didn't know I was – beautiful?

**CAT**. *(He has her now.)* Gorgeous. Exquisite.

**WOMAN**. Really?

**CAT**. A regular Venus.

**WOMAN**. Well. I will make a bargain with you. If I ever say one word in your praise, you may come into the Cave.

**CAT**. And if you say two words in my praise?

**MAN**. I never shall.

**CAT**. Never?

**WOMAN**. No. But if I do, you may sit by the fire in the Cave.

**CAT**. And if you say three words in my praise?

**WOMAN**. I never shall.

**CAT**. Never?

WOMAN. Never. But if I do, then you may drink the warm white milk three times a day for always and always and always. *(exit)*

CAT. *(to audience)* Now let everyone who hears this remember what the Wife of my Enemy has said. If she praises me – calls me an angel or clever, or wise, for instance – call out very loudly, "Cat! Cat!" Will you try it now with me?

*(Audience responds.* CAT *asks for repetition until he gets desired level of response.)*

Good. Don't forget. I shall go now and walk by myself. And while I do, please imagine that a whole year has passed away.

*(*CAT *exits. Lights dim. Suddenly* MAN *bursts onto the stage. He is wilder than ever, this time with joy. He "ho's" and "ha's" and dances around as the* ANIMALS *enter and watch, puzzled.* CAT *also enters and listens, off to one side. They ad lib to each other, "What is it? What's wrong?" Man's celebration reaches its peak, and he calls out joyfully.)*

MAN. A father! I'm a father! Dog, do you hear that? I'm a father!! Horse! Horse, what do you think? I'm a father! Cow, I'm a father! I'd give you all cigars but I haven't invented them yet!

DOG. What is a father?

MAN. *(A beat. He achieves a moment of pride and dignity.)* A real man. A civilized man. It means there is a new baby in the Cave. My wife is his Mother and I am his Father!

HORSE. What is a baby?

MAN. A little… *(He shows them with his hands.)* Well, he's new and soft and fat and small. And delicious to hold.

COW. Will he like us?

MAN. When he is bigger…yes, I think so. When he is bigger.

DOG. What does he like now?

**MAN.** Now? Now he likes things that are fuzzy, and tickle. He likes warm things to hold in his arms when he falls asleep. And he likes being played with. He likes all those things.

**CAT.** *(to audience)* Aha. That means my time has come.

**MAN.** But come, we have many things to do. Horse, Dog, we must hunt in earnest now. We have a family to care for. Cow, chew that cud! Work on that milk! Babies need milk. *(to audience)* We fathers are so important. Come on! *(They exit.)*

*(The* **WOMAN** *appears in the cave with baby, a doll. She snuggles him fondly, then puts him down by the cave entrance to play while she sweeps the cave floor. Crying is heard. She picks baby up and crying stops. She puts him down again. Crying again. She picks him up again, and crying stops. She tries to sweep while holding baby. Can't. She is frustrated for a moment, then takes him outside, sits him up by the cave and gives him pebbles to play with. Goes back into the cave. Baby cries some more. Woman continues to sweep, but the crying clearly bothers her.* **CAT** *now comes over to baby, in his purring-est humor. Pats baby on face. Crying stops. Tickles baby under chin. Baby coos.* **CAT** *continues to play with baby and we hear gurgles, giggles and other sounds of contentment.* **WOMAN** *hears it too, and her tension relaxes.)*

**WOMAN.** A blessing on whatever angel has made my baby stop crying!

*(***CAT** *cues the audience, if need be, until they cry out, "Cat! Cat!"* **WOMAN** *stops dead, then comes out of the cave.)*

Ooops – what have I said?

**CAT.** Good day, oh Wife of my Enemy! You have spoken a word in my praise, and now I can sit inside the cave for always and always.

**WOMAN.** Oh you…Cat! Be off with you.

*(She picks up baby and carries him inside. He immediately begins crying, and calls out, "Kitty! Kitty!")*

Oh – come in, then!

CAT. *(grandly)* Since you beg me to – very well.

> *(He enters, crosses to baby, who stops crying. He lies down beside baby, and baby falls asleep.)*

Now I will sing the Baby a song that will keep him asleep for an hour. *(CAT establishes a purr.)*

WOMAN. *(looking down on them)* That was wonderfully done. No question about it, you are a very clever cat.

> *(Again, CAT cues the audience if need be until they yell out, "Cat! Cat!")*

Oh no! What have I said?

CAT. You have said a second word in my praise, oh Wife of my Enemy. Now I can sit by the warm fire for always and always.

WOMAN. Oh, you…

CAT. *(quickly)* If I move, he wakes up!

WOMAN. *(ungraciously)* Oh, very well. You can sit by the fire.

CAT. Since I am so graciously invited…I accept.

WOMAN. BUT…You may be sure I shall NEVER say a third word in your praise, do what you will!

> *(She bustles about, sweeping angrily. The CAT suddenly spots a little mouse near the stew pot.)*

CAT. Oh, Woman – *(She ignores him.)* Oh, Woman –

WOMAN. To you I'm not speaking.

CAT. Oh, Woman, what goes into your stew pot?

WOMAN. Since you must know, Cat, it is wild oxtails and wild mushrooms broiled together with wild onions and wild herbs.

CAT. Oh, Woman, are you sure that one of your ingredients is not wild mouse?

WOMAN. Wild mouse? Yuk! Of course not! Whatever gave you that idea?

CAT. Because a mouse is sitting on the edge of your pot right now!

WOMAN. *(Loud shriek; she jumps away.)* Oh Cat, save me from the mouse!

CAT. I thought you needed no one else but Dog, Horse and
    Cow?

WOMAN. *(in a panic)* Oh, please, Cat, PLEASE!

CAT. *(bored)* If you insist.

   *(He gets up in a leisurely way, careful not to disturb
   baby. Then there is a creep, a pounce and a gobble.)*

WOMAN. *(greatly relieved)* A hundred thanks. Even the First
    Friend is not quick enough to catch little mice as you
    have done. You must be very wise.

   *("Cat! Cat!" business with the audience again.)*

CAT. Well, Wife of my Enemy, you have spoken a third
    word in my praise. Now I can drink the warm white
    milk three times a day for always and always.

WOMAN. *(Relaxes and laughs. She pours him some milk and
    sets it before him.)* Well, Cat, I see you are as clever as
    a Woman. But remember that your bargain was not
    made with the Man or the Dog. I do not know what
    they will do when they come home.

CAT. *(unconcernedly lapping his milk)* What does it matter
    about them?

WOMAN. Perhaps it doesn't matter, Cat. Who knows? But
    we will soon find out. I see them on their way now.
    *(looks off into the distance)* Come, Baby, *(She picks him up.)*
    we'll meet your Papa half way. *(to **DOG**, who has come
    bounding onstage)* Good Dog!

   *(The **WOMAN** exits as the **DOG** frisks into the cave.)*

DOG. Ha! I've beaten everyone! *(Notices **CAT**. Stops dead.)*
    What are you doing here?

CAT. I have a right to be here.

DOG. What right?

CAT. I have made a bargain with the Woman. She is a very
    clever Woman, Dog, but she is not as clever as I am.

DOG. What bargain?

CAT. I may come into the Cave. I may sit by the fire. And I
    may drink the warm white milk three times a day for
    always and always.

**DOG.** And in return?

**CAT.** I beg your pardon?

**DOG.** In return! What do you to earn your keep?

**CAT.** Do? Do? Am I a servant, like Horse and Cow and you? I do nothing, Dog. I do not hunt, or guard, or carry or give milk, as you peasants do. I am still the Cat who walks by himself.

**DOG.** *(He's had enough of this.)* Not when I am near, my clever Cat. When I am near, you will be the Cat who runs away!

**CAT.** *(hisses, back arches)* Says who?

**DOG.** These claws, Cat, and these great big teeth!

*(There is a great hissing and barking, and the DOG chases the CAT offstage, past the MAN and WOMAN who re-enter with the baby.)*

**MAN.** What was all that?

**WOMAN.** I think it was a lesson in being clever, my dear. You see, I am cleverer than the Dog. And the Cat, I am afraid, is cleverer than I am. But as it turns out, the Dog has outdone the clever Cat. Now how do you explain that?

**MAN.** *(It's too much for him.)* Who can explain it? What's for dinner?

**WOMAN.** *(as they exit)* Well, what did you bring home in your hunting bag?

**MAN.** *(It's an enormous bag.)* I have some wild pheasant with wild grouse and wild hedgehog, wild gasquantcha-wabas, wild kumquats, and just a tiny bit of wild persimmon, and for dessert, wild mangoes....

*(They are off. Upstage, the DOG and CAT chase through one more time.)*

### *THIRD SING-SONG OF OLD MAN KANGAROO*

**ACTOR #3.** Old Man Kangaroo, whatever will you do?

**ACTOR #5.** There he is on the banks of the Wallgong

**ACTOR #4.** Right where we left him on the edge of the river

**ACTOR #2.** With Yellow Dog Dingo ever getting nearer

**ALL.** And there isn't any bridge to cross! Up he stands on his BACK legs, his BACK legs

**ACTOR #3.** He stretches –

**ACTOR #5.** – and he stretches

**ACTOR #2.** – and the back legs getting longer

**ACTOR #4.** – and he HOPS across the river!

**ALL.** Guess he had to!

**ACTOR #5.** Hopping through Flinders

**ACTOR #4.** Hopping through cinders

**ACTOR #2.** Hopping through the deserts in the middle of Australia. He hops like a Kangaroo!

**ACTOR #5.** One yard –

**ALL.** Three yards – Five yards hopping

**ACTOR #3.** Look at his legs getting stronger and stronger

**ACTOR #4.** Look at his legs getting longer and longer

**ALL.** He hops like a Kangaroo!

**ACTOR #4.** Here comes Dingo, always running Dingo

**ACTOR #3.** Very much bewildered

**ACTOR #2.** Very much hungry

**ACTOR #5.** And wondering what in the world –

**ACTOR #4.** Or out of it –

**ACTOR #5.** Makes old Kangaroo hop!

**ACTOR #3.** Cause he hops like a cricket...

**ACTOR #2.** Like a pea in a saucepan –

**ACTOR #4.** Like a new rubber ball on a nursery floor!

**ACTOR #5.** And still comes Dingo

**ACTOR #2.** Tired-dog Dingo

**ACTOR #4.** Hungrier and hungrier

**ACTOR #5.** And wondering what in the world –

**ACTOR #4.** Or out of it –

**ALL.** Would make old Kangaroo stop!

**ACTOR #3.** Up rears Nqong from his bath in the salt pans, saying

**NQONG.** (ACTOR #2) It's five o'clock

**ACTOR #4.** Down sits Dingo

**ACTOR #5.** Poor-dog Dingo

**ACTOR #3.** Always hungry

**ACTOR #4.** Dusty in the sunshine

**ALL.** Hangs out his tongue and howls.

**ACTOR #5.** Down sits old man Kangaroo

**ACTOR #3.** Stretches out his long back legs

**ACTOR #4.** Scowls at the world and the great god Nqong

**ACTOR #3.** Scowls at Dingo

**KANGAROO.** – especially at Dingo –

**ACTOR #5.** And says –

**KANGAROO.** What did you do?

**NQONG.** Where are your manners, Kangaroo? Thank my
Dingo, tired dog Dingo, for what he's done for you.

**KANGAROO.** *Thank* that Dingo, yellow-dog Dingo?
*Thank* that Dingo with a mouth like a rat-trap?
He's chased me out of the homes of my childhood;
He's chased me out of my regular mealtimes;
He's changed my shape – and I'll never be the same
again –
And played Old Scratch with my legs!

**NQONG.** Maybe I'm wrong, but I seem to remember
A certain animal
A *pesty* animal
Disturbing me in my bath in the salt-pans
(*mimicking*) Make me different, and very much run
after,
And do it all by five this afternoon!
And now it is five o'clock!

**KANGAROO.** Yes, I know, and I wish I hadn't!
I thought you were going to make me a spell
And make me perfect, all by magic,
Not play a practical joke!

**NQONG.** Joke, you ungrateful bush-league jack-rabbit!
    JOKE! You stretched out piece of rag
    Say that again and I'll whistle up Dingo
    and run your hind legs off!

**KANGAROO.** Never mind, never mind, I apologize.
    Legs are legs, and they suit me fine.
    All I meant, oh mighty Lordliness, all I meant to say,
    your honor,
    Was I haven't eaten a thing since morning,
    And I'm very empty indeed.

**DINGO.** Empty, empty, talk about empty
    I've made him different,
    I've made him run after,
    What do *I* get to eat?

**NQONG.** Come and ask me about it tomorrow.
    For now, I must have a wash!

    *(Exit all but* **DINGO** *and* **KANGAROO.***)*

**DINGO.** Roo, roo, kangaroo!

**KANGAROO.** Dingo, Dingo!

**DINGO.** You stretched out rabbit!

**KANGAROO.** You dusty brat!

**DINGO.** It's your fault –

**KANGAROO.** Your fault!

**DINGO.** Your fault!

**KANGAROO.** Your fault!

**BOTH.** And that is that!

### THE CAMEL'S HASH IS SETTLED

    *(Bows at the end of third kangaroo sing-song.* **CAMEL**
    *wanders on, says "humph!" Both actors ad lib vigorous*
    *protests. Other actors enter and everyone talks at once,*
    *venting their anger on the* **CAMEL.** *Enter the* **DJINNI,**
    *who sweeps in and raises an imperious hand.)*

**DJINNI.** Silence. Silence! My friends, silence. This matter
    calls for a little finesse. (**DJINNI** *approaches* **CAMEL.**) My
    long and bubbling friend, what's this I hear of you?

**CAMEL.** Humph!

**DJINNI.** You've been most rude to your fellow animals, sneering and sneering at them. And besides, you're most 'scruciatingly idle. I've been searching for you for days.

**CAMEL.** Humph.

**DJINNI.** I shouldn't say that again if I were you. You might say it once too often. Bubbles, I want you to apologize.

**CAMEL.** Humph!

**DJINNI.** Now, Bubbles, I did warn you.

*(He takes off his cape and stuffs it down the* **CAMEL'S** *back.* **CAMEL** *cranes his neck around, is horrified, tries to shake it off and can't.)*

Do you see that? That's your very own humph that you've brought upon your very own self. Now you're coming home with me, to the Howling Desert, and settling down to work! And no more sneering!

**CAMEL.** How can I work with this humph on my back?

**DJINNI.** That's made on purpose. You will be able to work for three days without eating, because you can live on your humph. So don't say I never did anything for you. Come on now, Bubbles, apologize!

*(* **CAMEL** *looks sheepish – if such a thing is possible – and whispers in the* **DJINNI'S** *ear)*

He – says he can't. He says it goes against his nature… *(more whispering)* But he does want to be friends and begs you all to sing with him.

**ALL.** *(singing)* *

THE CAMEL'S HUMP IS AN UGLY LUMP
WHICH YOU MAY SEE AT THE ZOO,
BUT UGLIER YET, IS THE HUMP WE GET
FROM HAVING TOO LITTLE TO DO.
KIDDIES AND GROWNUPS TO-O-O-O-
IF WE HAVEN'T ENOUGH TO DO-O-O-O-

---

*For music see page 52.

GET THE HUMP, CAMELIOUS HUMP,
THE HUMP THAT IS BLACK AND BLUE!

WE CLIMB OUT OF BED WITH A FROUZLY HEAD,
AND A SNARLY-YARLY VOICE,
WE SHIVER AND SCOWL AND WE GRUNT AND GROWL
AT OUR BATH AND OUR BOOTS AND OUR TOYS.

AND THERE OUGHT TO BE A CORNER FOR ME
(AND I KNOW THERE IS ONE FOR YOU)
WHEN WE GET THE HUMP, CAMELIOUS HUMP
THE HUMP THAT IS BLACK AND BLUE!

**ALL.** *(cont.)*

THE CURE FOR THIS ILL IS NOT TO SIT STILL
OR FROWN WITH A BOOK BY THE FIRE,
BUT TO TAKE A LARGE HOE AND SHOVEL ALSO
AND DIG TILL YOU GENTLY PERSPIRE.
AND THEN YOU WILL FIND THAT THE SUN AND THE WIND
AND THE DJINN OF THE GARDEN TOO
HAVE LIFTED THE HUMP, THE HORRIBLE HUMP
THE HUMP THAT IS BLACK AND BLUE!
I GET IT AS WELL AS YOU-OO-OO
IF I HAVEN'T ENOUGH TO DO-OO-OO
WE ALL GET THE HUMP, CAMELIOUS HUMP
KIDDIES AND GROWNUPS TOO!


**The End**

# Just So

Words, Jan Silverman
Music, Louise King Lanzilotti

SCORE

MAN'S BEST FRIEND, WHO SLEEPS ON A CO - ZY SHELF WHILE THE MOUSE IS WO-MAN'S E - NE - MY AND THE
CAT JUST WALKS BY HIM - SELF? OH, HOW DID THE A - NI - MALS GET SO STRANGE BE - FORE THEY CAME TO THE
ZOO? I'VE GOT SOME EX - PLA - NA - TIONS, BUT THEY'RE NOT NE - CES - SA - RI - LY TRUE. I'LL
TELL YOU NOW IF YOU'LL COME WITH ME, MY TONGUE IS IN MY CHEEK. JUST LAST
WEEK IT ALL HAP - PENED JUST SO

# The Camel's Hump

# The Camel's Hump

# OTHER TITLES AVAILABLE FROM BAKER'S PLAYS

## THE JUNGLE BOOK

### Tracey Power

*TYA, Children's Theatre / 3m, 2f to play multiple roles / Simple Set*

Tracey Power's lively, youthful, and ultimately powerful adaptation of the Rudyard Kipling classic! *The Jungle Book* is the story of a boy abandoned to the jungle, Mowgli, who must learn to find his place within the longstanding community of animals. Taught by Baloo the bear, Bagheera the black panther, and Akela the old wolf, Mowgli is enlightened with the sacred master words of the hunting people: "We be of one blood, you and I." However, Shere Khan the tiger does not believe that Mowgli is part of the jungle only because he is a human. Mowgli must learn to abide by the ways of jungle law and stand up to the fierce Khan.

"There's something that just screams — and also howls, caws, roars, shrieks, hisses — theatre about the coming-of-age situation in which young Mowgli, the "man-cub" of Rudyard Kipling's celebrated *Jungle Book* stories, finds himself... *The Jungle Book* introduces a whole bunch of contemporary resonances — including ecological themes, the notion of belonging, [and] the folly of judging worth by appearance."
– *Edmonton Journal*

"Power has synthesized the stories into a clear and decisive one-act play."
– *The Gazette (Montreal)*

"The strength of the collective imagination is most definitely on display in Tracey Power's theatrical edition of *The Jungle Book*...the message of the importance of friends and family emerges effortlessly in this lush, colourful introduction to the ways of the jungle."
– *SEE Edmonton*

# OTHER TITLES AVAILABLE FROM BAKER'S PLAYS

## THREEE: THREE FUNNY FOLKTALES

### Colleen Neuman

*Folktales / Flexible casts of 9 to 31 / Simple sets*
Three very funny folktales from the author of our immensely popular
*PRINCESS PLAYS* and *LION AND MOUSE STORIES*.

### Winner! 2010 AATE Distinguished Play Award

***The Lion Who Roared*** – Lion's roaring is keeping the other animals in the jungle awake night after night. Zebra, Elephant, Leopard, Antelope and Hyena go to Lion and nervously request that he roar quietly. When Lion roars his refusal, Zebra announces that there is a new animal in the jungle that is bigger, stronger, louder than Lion. Lion, furious, challenges this Popalopalus to three contests to prove who is mightiest. Zebra runs home and confesses he made it up. There is no Popalopalus. So they use all the jungle animals to build one. When this creature wins all three contests, Lion stops roaring and starts whispering.

***A Fair Price*** – A cart driver is demanding that a woman pay him three copper coins for sitting in the shadow of his cart. A baker demands another woman pay three copper coins for smelling his honey cakes. A peddler requires a third woman to pay three copper coins when she overhears the music of a flute he demonstrates for a customer. All three women refuse to pay and take their cases to a wise woman who tells them they must pay a fair price. The first woman is told to pay the cart driver with the shadows of three copper coins. The second woman pays the baker with the smell of three copper coins. The third woman shakes three copper coins and pays the peddler with the sound of them rattling.

***Banana Sandwich In A Boat*** – A man and woman are about to be married when the groom announces that their firstborn child will be named Banana Sandwich In A Boat. The bride's father denounces him as a fool and calls off the wedding. The groom proposes that if he can find three people more foolish than himself the wedding will go on. The father agrees. First the groom finds a man so foolish that in order to put on his pants he climbs a tree, aims for the pants on the ground and jumps. Next he meets a woman who has built a house with no windows and is dumping buckets of sunshine into the house in order to get some light. Last, he finds a crowd arguing over how to get a woman riding a donkey into their village because the woman keeps banging her head on the archway over the gate. Half of them want to chop off the woman's head and the other half want to chop off the donkey's legs. The father sees that the groom is not nearly so foolish as the rest of the world and gives his blessing to the newlyweds.

# OTHER TITLES AVAILABLE FROM BAKER'S PLAYS

## ALL THE WORLDS A STAGE
### Seven Multi-cultural folktales

## Joann R. Leonard

*Casts 14-26 / Any flex-gender roles and female heroines / Simple production values suitable for stage or classroom*

Each play utilizes basic language phrases and axioms specific to the culture.

*The Riddle of the Tamborine* — a comedy from Spain where a court of madcap jesters serve a king with a misplaced funny bone.

*The Ring of Truth* — a morality play from West Africa in which two children discover their true inheritance with only a bag of kola Nuts.

*Quack, Quack, Stick to My Back!* — a farce from Italy where commedia characters romp from countryside to court in a zany procession.

*Wisdom for Sale* — an enterprising escapade from India where the aroma of pungent spices wafts from the colorful marketplace as two orphans earn rupees by selling their only possession, common sense.

*All the Wealth One Needs* — based on A Thousand and One Arabian Nights, this story within a story tells how a young woman's courage and intelligence saves the day.

*East or West, Home Is Best* — a Swedish tale of a haunted wood inhabited by a smorgasbord of trolls, witches and other forest creatures.

*The Great Bear of Orange* — a tale of romance from ancient Ireland in which a young girl must undergo perilous trials in order to come of age.